EVERYBODY'S WELCOME

For friends everywhere
—P.H.

For Susanne
—G.A.

All rights reserved. Published in the United States by Doubleday, an imprint of
Random House Children's Books, a division of Penguin Random House LLC, New York.
Originally published in the United Kingdom by Little Tiger Press, London, in 2017.

Doubleday and the colophon are registered trademarks of Penguin Random House LLC.

Visit us on the Web! rhcbooks.com

Educators and librarians, for a variety of teaching tools, visit us at RHTeachersLibrarians.com

Library of Congress Cataloging-in-Publication Data
Names: Hegarty, Patricia, author. | Abbott, Greg, illustrator.
Title: Everybody's welcome / Patricia Hegarty, Greg Abbott.
Other titles: Everybody is welcome
Description: First American edition. | New York : Doubleday Books for Young Readers, 2018. |
Summary: "When little Frog loses his home, Mouse decides they'll build a new one together. Soon
all the forest animals join in to build a home where everyone can be safe and warm."
—Provided by publisher.
Identifiers: LCCN 2017023228 | ISBN 978-1-5247-7165-2 (hc)
Subjects: | CYAC: Stories in rhyme. | Home—Fiction. | Belonging (Social psychology)—Fiction. |
Forest animals—Fiction. | Building—Fiction.
Classification: LCC PZ8.3.H3976 Eve 2017 | DDC [E]—dc23

MANUFACTURED IN CHINA
10 9 8 7 6 5 4 3 2 1
First American Edition

CPB/1800/0847/0118

EVERYBODY'S WELCOME

Patricia Hegarty

Greg Abbott

Doubleday Books
for Young Readers

In a forest clearing,
there is a little mouse,
dreaming of the future
in a great big happy house.

Suddenly, a frog appears with a sorry tale of woe:
"My pond, my home, is all dried up! I have no place to go."

"Froggy, please don't worry. You can stick with me.
Everything will be alright, just you wait and see."

"Let's build a home together.
We'll make it big and strong.
And once we get it started,
you won't be sad for long.

Everybody's welcome,
no matter who they are,
wherever they may come from,
whether near or far."

"Please help us!" cry the rabbits.
"We've had an awful scare.
 An eagle chased us from our home.
 Do you have room to spare?"

"Everybody's welcome
if you need a place to hide.
Come and help us build this house.
You'll all be safe inside."

"Some of us
can form a chain
and all work as a team.

We'll build a shelter
stick by stick,
following our dream."

"I'm all alone," cries big Brown Bear
with teardrops in his eyes.
"I frighten other people off
because of my great size."

"Come along and join us, Bear!
A great big guy like you
is just what we've been missing.
There's so much you can do!"

"Everybody's welcome,
and all can play their part.
Just look at big Brown Bear—
he's already made a start!"

Flapping and a-fluttering,
a flock of birds arrive.
"Someone chopped our tree down!
How *will* we all survive?"

"If we all work together,
no task is too great.
Even if some helpers
arrive a little late. . . ."

"Sorry I'm late."

"And the news will soon spread . . .

for miles
around . . .

of what
we are
building . . .

As the rain clouds gather
in a dark and stormy sky,
the animals keep building
a roof to keep them dry.

"When our house is ready
and everything's complete,
we'll all live here together
and life will be so sweet."

"Our home will be so happy,
and we'll fill it up with song.
Everyone who lives here
will know that they belong."

HOME
SWEET
HOME